Note to parents and carers

Many children are now taught to read using the phonic approach. This means they are taught to look at the letters, say the sounds, and then blend them to make a word. So, for example, children blend **c/a/t** to make the word **cat**, and **sh/o/p** to make **shop**.

When children have completed their initial phonics learning, they are ready to apply it to reading real books. Ladybird's **Superhero Phonic Readers** are planned for this exciting stage.

Some words are hard to read using beginner phonics. These words are often known as 'tricky words'. Some of these occur frequently in the English language so it is useful for children to memorize them.

Have fun doing our Tricky Words Memory Quiz on page 30. This features the most useful tricky words from the story.

How to use Superhero Phonic Readers:

⭐ Start at level one and gradually progress through the series. Each story is a little bit longer than the last and uses more grown-up vocabulary.

⭐ Children will be able to read **Superhero Phonic Readers** for themselves. Let your child read to you, and share the excitement!

⭐ If your child finds any words difficult, help him or her to work out the sounds in the word.

⭐ Early readers can be concentrating so hard on the words that they sometimes don't fully grasp the overall meaning of what they read. The puzzle questions on pages 28 and 29 will help with this. Have fun talking about them together.

⭐ There is a reward chart at the back of the book - young readers can fill this in and add stickers to it.

⭐ The Ladybird website **www.ladybird.com** features a wealth of information about phonics and reading.

⭐ Enjoy reading together!

Geraldine Taylor
Ladybird Educational Consultant

Educational Consultant: Geraldine Taylor
Phonics Consultant: Marj Newbury

A catalogue record for this book is available from the British Library

Published by Ladybird Books Ltd
80 Strand, London, WC2R 0RL
A Penguin Company

2 4 6 8 10 9 7 5 3 1
© LADYBIRD BOOKS LTD MMX
LADYBIRD and the device of a Ladybird are trademarks of Ladybird Books Ltd

ISBN: 978-1-40930-468-5

Printed in China

Superhero Phonic Readers

Sky Boy

written by Mandy Ross

illustrated by Mark Ruffle

Meet Sky Boy.

He flies like a plane. He swoops like a bird.

Sky Boy is a hero of the sky.

Look out, Sky Boy!
Here is Captain Badman, the Sky Pirate.
Captain Badman looks for gold.

Oh, no! Captain Badman is robbing the Air Ship.

"Give me the gold," says Captain Badman,
"or I will push you over the side."

"Sky Boy!" shouts the air-sailor.
"We need your help!"

"On my way," shouts Sky Boy. "It looks like
Captain Badman is up to his old tricks."

Sky Boy swoops over to help.

He fires a sky dart at Captain Badman's hot air balloon.
"Help! Save me!" calls Captain Badman.

"Captain Badman is a bad man," thinks Sky Boy.
"But shall I save him?"

"I will pay you with gold!" calls Captain Badman.

But he stole that gold from the Air Ship!

Sky Boy swoops down low.

"Yes, I will save you," says Sky Boy.

"Take my hand."

Then Sky Boy swoops high up in the sky with Captain Badman.

"You saved my life, Sky Boy," gasps Captain Badman. "But where are we going now? My home is that way."

"You will see," says Sky Boy.

The Air Ship
is this way.

"Oh, no!" says Captain Badman.
"You are taking me to the Air Ship."

"Oh, yes!" says Sky Boy.
"You must give back the gold."

Grumpy Captain Badman gives back the gold.
"I am sorry," he mutters.

"You will be!" says Sky Boy.
He gives a signal.

"Oh, no!" gasps Captain Badman.
"Not the Sky Police!"

"Oh, yes, Captain Badman," say the Sky Police.

"Well done, Sky Boy!" say the Sky Police.
"You saved Captain Badman and the gold.
Now we can put him in jail."

"Hooray for Sky Boy!" everybody cheers.

Superhero Secret Puzzles

⭐ How does Sky Boy get around?

⭐ Is Captain Badman a good man?

⭐ Who does the gold belong to?

⭐ Where will the Sky Police take Captain Badman?

⭐ Do you think Sky Boy should have saved Captain Badman?

⭐ If you could fly like Sky Boy, where would you fly?

Look at these pictures from the story and say the order they should go in.

A

B

C

D

Answer on page 30.

Tricky Words Memory Quiz

Can you remember these words from the story?

See if you can read them super-fast.

he

the

out

oh

no

me

I

you

we

your

to

where

are

going

be

What else can you remember?

Can you put the book down and say what happens in the story?

The answer to the picture puzzle on page 29 is: B, C, D, A.

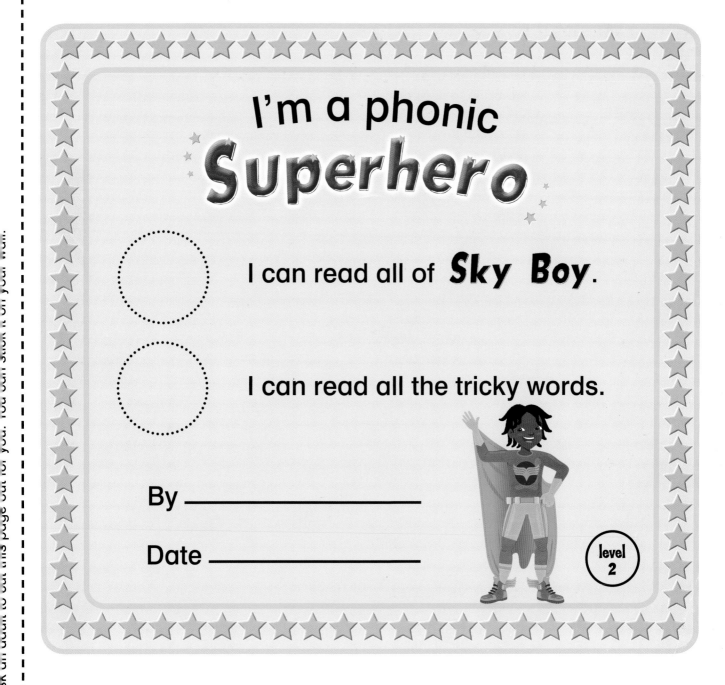

I'm a phonic
Superhero

I can read all of **Sky Boy**.

I can read all the tricky words.

By _____

Date _____

level
2